M000016928

A Lifetime Burning

by Cusi Cram

FOUNDED 1830

NEW YORK HOLLYWOOD LONDON TORONTO

SAMUELFRENCH.COM

ISBN 978-0-573-69828-6   Printed in U.S.A.   #29267

MUSIC USE NOTE

Licensees are solely responsible for obtaining formal written permission from copyright owners to use copyrighted music in the performance of this play and are strongly cautioned to do so. If no such permission is obtained by the licensee, then the licensee must use only original music that the licensee owns and controls. Licensees are solely responsible and liable for all music clearances and shall indemnify the copyright owners of the play and their licensing agent, Samuel French, Inc., against any costs, expenses, losses and liabilities arising from the use of music by licensees.

IMPORTANT BILLING AND CREDIT
REQUIREMENTS

All producers of *A LIFETIME BURNING must* give credit to the Author of the Play in all programs distributed in connection with performances of the Play, and in all instances in which the title of the Play appears for the purposes of advertising, publicizing or otherwise exploiting the Play and/or a production. The name of the Author *must* appear on a separate line on which no other name appears, immediately following the title and *must* appear in size of type not less than fifty percent of the size of the title type.

In addition the following credit *must* be given in all programs and publicity information distributed in association with this piece:

Originally developed with LAByrinth Theatre Company

World Premiere produced by Primary Stages, August 2009

A LIFETIME BURNING was first produced by Primary Stages in New York City on July 28, 2009. The performance was directed by Pam MacKinnon, with sets by Kris Stone, costumes by Theresa Squire, lighting by David Weiner, and sound design by Broken Chord Collective. The cast was as follows:

TESS. . . . . Christina Kirk

EMMA . . . . .Jennifer Westfeldt

LYDIA . . . . Isabel Keating

ALEJANDRO . . . . Raúl Castillo

CHARACTERS

TESS – late 30s
EMMA – late 30s
ALEJANDRO – early twenties, Latino
LYDIA – 40s, British

EDITOR'S NOTE

Home is where one starts from. As we grow older
The world becomes stranger, the pattern more complicated
Of dead and living. Not the intense moment
Isolated, with no before and after,
But a lifetime burning in every moment
And not the lifetime of one man only
But of old stones that cannot be deciphered.

– *T.S. Eliot,* East Coker

(A well renovated and thoughtfully designed studio apartment on the lower east side of Manhattan on Mulberry Street.)

(It's the kind of place that rents for $3800 a month. It's clean in a way most New York apartments are not; the cleanliness comes from the newness of everything.)

(The apartment is tastefully decorated in a minimalist, mid-century modern way. Everything in the space is well-curated and carefully placed.)

(The walls are white but a perfect, not glaring white, white maybe with a touch of ice blue or very light pink.)

(Lights come up on **TESS**. *She holds a newspaper in her hand. She shakes the newspaper at* **EMMA**.*)*

TESS. I can't. I can't. I can't. /I can't.

EMMA. /Since when do you have a stutter?

*(***TESS** *looks like she might hit* **EMMA** *with the newspaper.)*

TESS. You're off your meds.

EMMA. Maybe you need a prescription.

TESS. I mean. What. What. What. /WHAT?

EMMA. /Again with the repeating of/words

TESS. /This makes sense. More sense if you are.

EMMA. What makes sense?

TESS. Don't.

EMMA. Ask questions?

TESS. It's just. It's just. It's just.

EMMA. I'm concerned about this speech impediment.

TESS. *(calmly)* I would like an explanation. Detailed. Comprehensive.

EMMA. Comprehensive?

TESS. I am asking the questions, Emma. No tactics.

EMMA. Tactics?

TESS. I want an EXPLANATION.

EMMA. I think what you really want is an EXPLICATION.

TESS. No word games. I hate the word/games

EMMA. /Explication is more of an interpretation. More detailed.

TESS. I would appreciate details.

EMMA. Like an "*explication du texte.*" That's where you go through the text word by word, parse every last syllable.

TESS. You're evading.

EMMA. I'm EXPLICATING.

TESS. Details. Facts. WHY! WHY!/WHY!

EMMA. /I thought this might irk you.

TESS. Thought? Might? Irk? IRK/ is what someone who bumps into you on the subway does.

EMMA. /But I didn't think fireworks would ensue. Interesting.

(**TESS** *throws the newspaper to the ground.*)

TESS. I have an ethical obligation!

EMMA. I didn't know that "Luxurious Homes" magazine had a code of journalistic ethics?

TESS. I am your sister and I am responsible for you.

EMMA. I'm not five, Tess.

TESS.	**EMMA.**
I'm a journalist for fucking fuck's sake.	You write about wallpaper and fancy paperweights

TESS. At least I HAVE a job.

(**TESS** *walks away from* **EMMA**. *She picks up The New York Times.*)

TESS. *(cont.)* Shall we just take a moment to peruse?

*(***TESS*** *opens the paper.)*

It's you. Your picture. In The New York Times. On the COVER of the Thursday "STYLE" section! Look, there you are, *(to picture)* "Hello, Emma," talking about the upcoming publication of your heart rending MEMOIR. In this VERY apartment. *(***TESS*** *looks around.)* And what is up with the apartment? Last time I was here, it was milk crate and futon central. What the fuck is going on?

EMMA. Calm down, Tess.

TESS. No. No. No. I will not be calm until. Until. Until. Until, I can wrap my head around THIS lunacy, this aberration, this, this calum...calum...FUCK HOW DO YOU SAY IT!

EMMA.	**TESS.**
Calumny. Is the accent on the first part of the word...CALumny? Or is it, calUMNY?	Fuck the word. Just fuck it. Fuck you. It's a fucking fucked up disaster, is what it is.

EMMA. It's a story. You always liked stories.

TESS. WHY!

EMMA. You were always a sucker for a "tall tale."

TESS. Bottom line it, Emma.

EMMA. A "gothic yarn."

TESS. You CANNOT masquerade fiction as TRUTH.

EMMA. And I would answer to that, "what is truth"?

TESS. No polemics, you didn't finish college.

EMMA. In this day and age is there an objective, or indeed absolute truth?

TESS. It's always the people without DEGREES that throw philosophy at you.

EMMA. Wanna Gibson?

TESS. No. No. No. I do not want a GIBSON. I want an escape hatch from the nightmare of being related to you!

EMMA. Cocktail hour just arrived early!

(**EMMA** *gets up and goes to her stainless steel kitchen and takes out the ingredients for a Gibson. She takes vodka out of the freezer. She pulls vermouth from a cabinet. She finds a shaker and ice crusher. She carefully measures vodka and vermouth into the shaker.*)

(**TESS** *looks at her Blackberry and shakes her head. She dials.*)

TESS. *(into the phone)* No. No. No. No ice cream. *(a pause)* I am NOT being tyrannical, or...or...like Hitler. Because...because you are lactose intolerant. Have Marisol get you some Rice Dream. I know it's unfair but Harry isn't lactose intolerant and I cannot have this conversation again. Talk to you at bed time.

(**TESS** *hangs up.*)

EMMA. Since when is Charlotte lactose intolerant?

TESS. Don't pretend you know anything about Charlotte.

(**EMMA** *leans in to her fridge and pulls out cocktail onions.* **TESS** *eyes Emma's coffee table. She taps it, then kicks the leg. She gets on her knees and looks underneath the table.*)

TESS. This is vintage Eva Zeisel!

EMMA. You're good.

TESS. Where did you get this?

EMMA. E-bay.

TESS. Don't lie to me.

EMMA. Don't worry, Mom didn't leave me a secret table in a secret will you never read.

TESS. That's like three thousand dollars of coffee table.

EMMA. More. It's the larger size.

(**EMMA** *smashes the ice with an old fashioned ice breaker and adds it into the shaker.*)

TESS. How much did you get?

EMMA. For what?

(**EMMA** *shakes the cocktail shaker.*)

TESS. How much?

EMMA. Enough to INVEST in a few things.

TESS. *(taking in the surroundings)* Ok. Ok. I spy with my little eye, two Globus chairs, a Saarinen Pedestal table, a custom ottoman re-upholstered in a hip FEMININE fabric. Sofa. Definitely from Design within Reach.

*(*TESS *sits on the sofa. She bounces.)*

Funny, how comfy sitting on a pack of LIES is.

EMMA. They're LIFE pieces.

TESS. Who's life?

*(*EMMA *shakes the cocktail shaker.)*

Sofa and ottoman, lets say six thousand with delivery fees, reupholstering another two grand. Was the fabric expensive?

EMMA. Italian.

TESS. Lets just round it up to ten grand. *(taking in more of the room)* And THEN. The Kitchen. The paint job. The floors. You dropped a hundred thousand on this place. And I'm lowballing. You sold your book for at least a quarter of a million! *(beat)* Good, all this stuff has re-sale value.

*(*EMMA *pours her Gibson into a martini glass.)*

EMMA. I think I'm becoming a drunk-o-rexic.

TESS. What?

EMMA. Girls who drink and don't eat. I've been cutting down on the eating because of the book tour.

TESS. You're not going on a book tour.

EMMA. My editor sent me this study, I think it was on Gawker, that thinner writers sell more books. Like that woman who wrote the eating/praying/living book – REALLY thin.

TESS. Kill me now.

EMMA. Must be the stress…

TESS. Of lying?

EMMA. I find that word reductive.

TESS. You said you were part INCA.

EMMA. I could be part Inca. It's possible.

(**EMMA** *sips her Gibson and adds some more vermouth.*)

TESS. No it isn't, not possible. You're Irish. One hundred
percent. Both sides. Not even English. Or Scottish. Just
"top o the morning, potato munching" Irish.

EMMA. Maybe I feel part Inca?

TESS. What. What. What…could that possibly mean?

(**EMMA** *puts the cocktail onions away and pops a few in
her mouth.*)

EMMA. Are cocktail onions caloric? The camera adds ten
pounds so I figure if I'm twenty pounds under my
comfortable weight, on camera I'll look ten pounds
too thin – or skinny which is all anyone wants to be
in this fine country of ours. (*She raises her glass.*) Chin.
Chin.

(**EMMA** *sits.*)

How are the twins? The almost ex? The Puggle?

(**TESS** *gets up and goes to the freezer pulls out the bottle
of vodka and pours a large amount of it into a glass.
She smashes a tray of ice into the sink and plops several
cubes into her glass.*)

TESS. Vermouth is sixty calories a shot. That was a very gen-
erous pour. You double dipped. Adds up. Especially if
you are on a liquid diet.

EMMA. Are you "counting points" again? Because you look
thinner.

TESS. In the future when you are trying to compliment
someone, just say you look thin. The ER takes the
compliment away.

(*They sip their drinks.*)

TESS. *(cont.)* So…I'm very curious how exactly you feel Incan? Or I believe in the article it said you were a quarter Inca and a quarter Cherokee. Just couldn't be indigenous from one hemisphere, had to take on the plight of two native peoples?

EMMA. There was also some mention of my other "Irish" half.

TESS. Funny, how that slipped my mind. I guess I was just absorbing so much new information, the true stuff didn't register. I'm all ears.

EMMA. Well…I've had this job for the last three years…

TESS. I thought you were volunteering a couple of hours a week.

EMMA. Ten hours a week. And I treated it like a job.

TESS. That's not a job. Go on.

EMMA. Anyway, at my volunteer JOB, I tutored and mentored at risk Latino youth.

TESS. I have a cleaning lady from Honduras but I remain Irish. I am not even a tenth Honduran.

EMMA. A lot of the kids I work with are of South American descent, from Ecuador and Peru. And I got to know them and they seemed really…kindred.

TESS. Kindred?

EMMA. They're struggling with similar…issues

TESS. Like whether to spring for an original Eames chair or settle for the knock-off?

EMMA. This is pointless, Tess.

TESS. Please, I am aching to know what makes you feel "kindred" with at risk Latino youths.

EMMA. Well.

(**EMMA** *sips her Gibson.*)

A feeling of displacement.

TESS. How are you displaced?

EMMA. I don't feel like its possible for me to thrive in this culture. I live perpetually outside of it.

TESS. You were on the cover of the Style section today. That's pretty inside things.

EMMA. I'm talking about my connection to these kids. I shared a sense of profound alienation with them. I think it's that essential quality that is at the root of my...you know issues.

TESS. You mean, illness.

EMMA. Terminology.

TESS. So...let me get this straight, because you share a general sense of malaise with some South American kids, through some magical power of transference, you miraculously became Inca-ish.

EMMA. It's much more complex than that, Tess.

TESS. Then EXPLICATE it to me.

EMMA. I just wanted voices like theirs to be heard.

TESS. Can't they write their own books?

EMMA. No. They can't and that is the very heart of the problem. No amount of tutoring I do, is going to empower them enough to tell their stories to a wider audience.

TESS. So, you are in essence speaking for a speechless population?

EMMA. I wouldn't phrase it like that. Through my book, maybe my readers will see that difference is a social construct, it exists in the mind. And perhaps if we dig deep enough, we all have a little Inca in us.

TESS. And a little Cherokee?

EMMA. Do you know the percentage of native kids with juvenile diabetes?

TESS. No I don't, Emma. But I do know enough about native South Americans to know that they call themselves Quechua, not Incan.

EMMA. You sure about that?

TESS. Positive. My editor at "Luxurious Homes" is FULLY and REALLY a first generation Peruvian with REAL Quechua blood running through her veins, not Irish American blood posturing

as-all-the-oppressed-indigenous-peoples-of-the-world
blood. And FYI, you are lecturing me about diabetes
and natives peoples from a five thousand dollar sofa.

EMMA. You're just obstinate in your desire to not be able
to imagine a life different from your own suburban
nightmare, Tess.

(**EMMA** *get up and picks up the phone.*)

Sushi?

TESS. Absolutely not!

EMMA. Hola Ernesto, yeah the usual but no maki combo.
Rice makes me gorda. Ha. *(She looks at* **TESS.***)* And an
extra mixed sashimi. Si. Mi hermana. Bueno y COM-
PLICADO. Gracias to you, Ernesto.

(**TESS** *charges toward the phone and takes it out of*
EMMA *'s hands and speaks into it.*)

TESS. Yeah. Hey, Ernesto. Cancel that order. Mi HERMANA
has been a very bad girl and doesn't get sushi today.
Adios.

EMMA. Jesus Christ, Tess! I'm hungry.

TESS. I thought you were a DRUNK-O-REXIC?

TESS. How long have you been off your meds?

EMMA. Why am I the only one who has to answer questions?

TESS. Because this seems like a manic bender of EPIC pro-
portions.

TESS. Are you, or are you not taking your meds?

(**EMMA** *grabs the bottle of vodka out of the fridge. She
holds it up to* **TESS***;* **TESS** *nods yes.*)

EMMA. I'm on a new pill.

(She refreshes both of their glasses.)

TESS. Well, we should sue the fuck out of the company that
makes it.

EMMA. We live in a world where passion is medicated.

TESS. I can't have this discussion again.

EMMA. Good, because this discussion depresses me more than my depression.

(Both sisters take a swig of vodka. **EMMA** *winces.)*

EMMA. How can you drink this stuff straight?

TESS. Why didn't you talk to me about this, Emma?

EMMA. Seems like the twins always have strep.

TESS. I'm sorry...I wasn't more...the last six months have been...

EMMA. Don't. Please. It doesn't suit you. I didn't tell anyone, really. The whole thing was muy complicado. I needed to write something.

TESS. Why not write a novel?

EMMA. Memoirs sell better. Fiction isn't real enough anymore.

TESS. That makes no sense.

EMMA. I agree with you.

TESS. You're like a...maze...a maze inside a thimble. You can't pretend to be a race...a race that is not your own. It's racist.

EMMA. Is it?

TESS. Yes.

EMMA. But isn't my imagining what it would be like to be a quarter Cherokee and a quarter Inca...or rather Quechua, doesn't my desire to understand that reality transcend race?

TESS. Race is not transcendable. Race is a fact.

EMMA. Is it?

TESS. Don't look at me, I'm not Cornell West.

EMMA. It was just the way I wanted to tell that particular story.

TESS. I don't even know how I feel about people writing about worlds, even fictionally, that they barely know. It seems... presumptuous and smacking of fakery.

EMMA. You did NOT just say smacking of fakery?

TESS. Isn't art truth?

EMMA. Art is beauty.

TESS. Fine. *(beat)* I think beauty is truth.

EMMA. How Greco-Roman of you.

TESS. Why are truth and beauty so elusive?

EMMA. 'Cause they don't matter anymore.

TESS. THAT makes me want to string somebody up by the BALLS and make them ACCOUNTABLE.

EMMA. You're a buzzkill, Tess.

TESS. You and my almost ex are on the same page about that.

(The sisters drink.)

EMMA. I know that world.

TESS. After ten hours a week?

EMMA. For three years.

(silence)

EMMA. There is another story, Tess.

TESS. Always is with you.

EMMA. A story I didn't tell.

TESS. A true story?

EMMA. Some stories are too true to tell.

TESS. Tell me.

*(Lights comes up on **ALEJANDRO**. He sits at a table. He listens to his iPod while doing exercises in a workbook. He tries to write but gets lost in the beat of what he is listening to. He taps the table with his hand. Throughout the following he drums on the table.)*

EMMA. Alejandro made me laugh. It was that simple. Or complicated. He was oddly joyful, in spite of his circumstances. I was only supposed to tutor him once a week but there was no way he would ever pass his GED without more time, so I started meeting him for extra sessions at a coffee shop near the center. I wasn't supposed to have outside contact with my clients and I never did. Not before Alejandro.

(**EMMA** *gets up and plops down beside the table next to* **ALEJANDRO**.)

ALEJANDRO. Hola, Emma-lemma. You're late. I'm like all fucked up about these antonyms.

EMMA. I saw how hard you were working.

(**ALEJANDRO** *puts an ear piece in* **EMMA***'s ear and in his ear. He sings really loud.*)

ALEJANDRO. Check it out. Boricua, morena, dominicano, colombiano, boricua, morena, cubano, mexicano!

(**EMMA** *takes the ear piece out.*)

EMMA. OK. What specifically don't you get about antonyms?

ALEJANDRO. What no chatting? I like my little *bochinche* with my fine tutor before I strain my brain.

EMMA. Come on, Alejandro.

ALEJANDRO. So it's like all bizness and no playness?

EMMA. I was just working with Berto and...

ALEJANDRO. That dude is dumb.

EMMA. I don't like that word.

ALEJANDRO. How 'bout "challenged"? Like that word?

EMMA. Better. Berto's dyslexic and has never been given the correct therapies.

ALEJANDRO. And he's crazy dumb.

EMMA. Alejandro.

ALEJANDRO. Come on, I know no one can be retarded any more but Berto, he's like...the opposite of quick.

EMMA. Antonym. Slow is an antonym of quick.

ALEJANDRO. So you're admitting Berto is slow?

EMMA. No I am not...at all. I was...

ALEJANDRO. Come on. Admit it Emma, a chunk of Berto's cerebral cortex is on permanent leave.

(**EMMA** *stifles a smile and looks at* **ALEJANDRO***'s workbook.*)

EMMA. So…the common mistake people make with this section is to give up if they don't immediately know the word in capital letters.

ALEJANDRO. Know another common mistake people make these days is they let people off the hook. You can't just be dumb, you're like dyslexic or ADDish, or "special" or "challenged." Why can't people just fess up and admit they got problems. Wanna know what I am?

EMMA. What, Alejandro?

ALEJANDRO. Lazy. And as far as I can see, there is no treatment, or pill or special term for that but in this neighborhood it's an epidemic.

EMMA. I don't think that's the case.

ALEJANDRO. I know it is. You know how many hours there are in a week? 168. So my stupid job takes up 35 hours outta 168. Then, I sleep like 49 of those hours. And then there are like 84 hours every week where I'm basically doing dip shit. I mean, nada. I am like staring at the wall thinking about how many hours a week I do nothing. That's pathetic. I'm just gonna say it out loud…I am a lazy motherfucker.

EMMA. I don't think you're lazy.

ALEJANDRO. You know what my ancient peeps did with their free time?

EMMA. Uh…Built Machu Picchu? Got slaughtered?

ALEJANDRO. In between all that, they invented brain surgery and built roads from Colombia all the way down to the bottom of Chile. What have I invented? Or built?

EMMA. I mean…that was a different time.

ALEJANDRO. Yeah, like there were no cell phones, or electricity OR cars and like some Inca dude still thought about how to fucking drill a hole in someone's head.

EMMA. You can't let history get you down, Alejandro. You do a lot.

ALEJANDRO. What?

EMMA. You spend three hours a week with me.

ALEJANDRO. That's different.

EMMA. You wanna take the GED, so you can get a better job.

ALEJANDRO. Like I'll ever be a brain surgeon?

EMMA. Who knows? If we look to the power of the antonym, it could happen.

ALEJANDRO. What do you with your 84 hours?

EMMA. I have more than 84 hours. I don't sleep much.

ALEJANDRO. You have another job, right – I mean, this tutoring is like a volunteer job, right? Wait, let me guess. Maybe you work at the Metropolitan Museum, you like give tours all about old statues, or buy paintings at auctions...or...like you're in charge of kick ass parties, where everyone is in fucking ball gowns and like Angelina Jolie kisses your ass.

EMMA. I wish Angelina Jolie would kiss my ass.

ALEJANDRO. Mine too. Those big fat juicy lips...what I wouldn't give for an ass hicky from Angelina.

(**EMMA** *laughs.* **ALEJANDRO** *laughs. A moment.*)

ALEJANDRO. So what do you do...with your extra hours?

EMMA. Oh...it's not very interesting, whereas ANTONYMS are riveting.

ALEJANDRO. Tell me.

EMMA. I worry.

ALEJANDRO. For a living?

EMMA. If that were a job, I'd be a billionaire.

ALEJANDRO. So...what do you do, for real?

EMMA. Um. Well...I don't have a job per se at the moment. I have had jobs in the past. I worked as an underling at a fashion magazine, which was a not so subtle form of torture. Then at a non-profit which was stressful. I had to raise money – no skills in that arena. It's not really my forte, holding down a job.

ALEJANDRO. So...like your parents are rich?

EMMA. My parents are dead.

ALEJANDRO. Man, I'm sorry.

EMMA. Being an orphan has its perks.

ALEJANDRO. Like what?

EMMA. Life insurance. My dad left me some extra money. Drives my sister nuts. I told her I would split it with her but I think she would rather be angry than rich. She is rich, but my money seems better than hers.

ALEJANDRO. So you don't have to work?

EMMA. Not at the moment. If I continue to be unemployable and live in Manhattan, I will eventually run out of money. It's one of the things I worry about.

ALEJANDRO. Wow.

EMMA. Yeah.

ALEJANDRO. So you're loaded?

EMMA. No.

(a long, uncomfortable pause)

When I'm not feeling wretched about myself and how lazy I am and how pointless my life has become, I figure I lost both my parents when I was sixteen within eight months of each other, so...

ALEJANDRO. So?

EMMA. So...it's what I got instead of parents, money.

ALEJANDRO. My brother was shot but no one wrote me a check.

EMMA. I'm lucky, Alejandro. I squander my luck.

ALEJANDRO. What does squander mean?

EMMA. To waste. I waste my luck and time.

ALEJANDRO. Yeah.

EMMA. Can I ask you favor?

ALEJANDRO. Sure.

EMMA. Just keep what I told you to yourself. I just...if the other students...I dunno.

ALEJANDRO. I get it. No problem.

EMMA. Thanks.

(a beat)

ALEJANDRO. After Luis got shot, I was all like, I can't ever let anything like this happen again to my mom. And I gotta be a man and every day is gonna be all precious and shit. And I got my stupid-ass job and signed up at the center for tutoring. And like I try to avoid trouble and all, no matter what and that means hanging out a lot by myself. Cause in the old days if there was trouble within a five block radius, I would be like humping it. But even after the world comes down around you and you think you're all reborn and shit, you're not, you're still the fucked up lazy you, staring at the wall counting hours until the next thing you don't want to do.

(**EMMA** *begins to cry. She sobs.*)

ALEJANDRO. Hey, it's not so bad. At least you don't gotta work at Best Buy.

EMMA. *(crying)* Freedom is overrated.

ALEJANDRO. I could get you a job at Best Buy. My cousin is a manager.

EMMA. *(crying harder)* That's so sweet.

ALEJANDRO. You've obviously never been in a Best Buy.

EMMA. No.

ALEJANDRO. Thought so.

(**ALEJANDRO** *hands* **EMMA** *some napkins.*)

I don't like to see a pretty girl's face all wrecked. Breaks my heart.

EMMA. Sorry.

ALEJANDRO. It's OK. *(beat)* I'm kinda glad you don't like work at the Metropolitan Museum. I mean, I'm glad you told me, you know...

EMMA. I'm a sucky tutor.

ALEJANDRO. Nah uh.

EMMA. In the training they tell us to limit the details of our personal lives, to stay focused on task-based activities.

ALEJANDRO. It's not your fault I'm not into ant-o-boring-nyms.

EMMA. There gonna be on the GED. I want you to pass the GED. You should go to college.

ALEJANDRO. Did you?

EMMA. For a year and a half. But do the opposite of what I did, you'll be happy that way.

ALEJANDRO. Stop.

EMMA. Alejandro, I've worked with a lot of kids in the last three years and I try, I try to be hopeful and encouraging to them but the truth is, I look at a lot of them and I don't see their futures. But I look at you and see… possibility.

(ALEJANDRO smiles. A moment.)

ALEJANDRO. So do you like have friends?

EMMA. I'm not a total loser.

ALEJANDRO. I know, I just wonder what you do with them?

EMMA. We go to movies, sometimes the theater, sometimes bars. The ones that live in Brooklyn invite me to dinner parties. I try to avoid those.

ALEJANDRO. You ever go dancing?

EMMA. No. I mean, not in forever.

ALEJANDRO. You like to dance?

EMMA. Yeah…if I'm in the mood.

ALEJANDRO. When are you in the mood?

EMMA. It's been a long time.

ALEJANDRO. For me, it's when I feel like I could scream at the top of my lungs for hours and like if someone got just a little too close, I might punch them in the eye, know what I mean?

EMMA. I really do, actually. I am known for my sudden bursts of energy.

ALEJANDRO. It's funny.

EMMA. What?

ALEJANDRO. We're not so different.

(A pause. EMMA looks through ALEJANDRO's workbook.)

EMMA. Maybe we should skip antonyms for now. Let's do some analogies. They're hard, really hard for people who think creatively, you have to narrow down the way you make connections.

ALEJANDRO. Let's fuck it. Let's go dancing.

*(Lights begin to dim on **ALEJANDRO** and **EMMA**. **EMMA** gets up and watches **ALEJANDRO** leave.)*

*(Lights rise on **TESS**. **TESS**' cell phone rings – it's the theme from "9 to 5". It is loud, very loud.)*

EMMA. THAT'S your ring?

TESS. It's ironic.

EMMA. Barely.

*(**TESS** looks at her phone.)*

TESS. Fuck. It's Steve. He has the twins. You're so not done. *(on the phone – she speaks in a controlled monotone)* What? Yes. Yes. Yes. I'm with her. In her apartment. None of your business. I don't care, I really don't care about how anything affects you anymore. Yes I did say that and I did mean it. What do you want? *(pause)* How did that happen? Were they unsupervised? Where's Marisol? And Mrs. Pierce? I have told you countless times. I know. I know. I know. She loves grapes. I'll give you Dr. Fineman's number. He'll prescribe something an emetic or laxative…I can't remember. Of course I have told them not feed her grapes. Know what? Know what? Know what? *(the monotone goes out the window)* Ever think that maybe it's your FUCKING fault too. They have half your DNA, MOTHERFUCKER! *(beat, cool as a cucumber)* Dr. Fineman's number is 212-884-2181

*(**TESS** hangs up.)*

The twins fed the puppy grapes.

EMMA. Oh.

TESS. They know grapes are poisonous to Puggles. It's not the first time.

EMMA. Yikes.

TESS. They're acting out.

EMMA. Apparently.

TESS. I worry.

EMMA. Of course.

TESS. The divorce has been hard on them. Seven is a difficult age, you're old enough to understand but not old enough to have empathy. I just wish someone could display a soupcon of empathy. So what the fuck happened with Alejandro?

EMMA. I want to know what the fuck happened with Steve.

TESS. Well. Steve is an asshole.

EMMA. Well, yes.

TESS. I knew he was an asshole when I married him but he was my asshole.

EMMA. What's the distinction?

TESS. Between what?

EMMA. Your own asshole and an asshole that is not your own? I mean, you know what I mean…

TESS. Steve hired a barracuda of a divorce lawyer who's trying to paint him as the most destitute hedge fund manager on Wall Street. He wants full custody, so he can spoil the twins to death his new LOFT in Tribeca which has a ping pong table and satellite everything, in addition to a nanny AND a personal chef—how can I possibly compete with that? He wants to have the children, so he doesn't have to pay me to take care of them, even though I only employ one measly au pair and I don't even have cable – on principle, mind you. The idea of giving me any money whatsoever to raise his children makes him crazy. Why? Why? Why you ask?

EMMA. I didn't ask.

TESS. Yes you did.

EMMA. I asked a different question.

TESS. Why? Why? I'll tell you why. Because he is an asshole at large, learning new asshole tricks every day and making me pay for whatever his asshole Mom and Dad did to him to make him an asshole in the first place.

EMMA. I'm sorry, Tess.

TESS. He's not an asshole to the kids. I'm fine.

EMMA. How is that possible?

TESS. What are my options? Fall apart? Lose my kids? Lose my job? My house? End up in the nut house macrameing my life away? No thanks. No offence.

(The tinkle of ice in empty glasses.)

EMMA. I wonder what you say about me behind my back.

TESS. Most people don't spend that much time thinking about other people, Emma.

EMMA. Still.

TESS. We are the stars of our own stupid movies.

EMMA. So, I'm just a walk on in your movie?

TESS. If only. *(beat)* So, you and Alejandro went dancing. And…he made you an honorary Inca?

EMMA. The story doesn't go in order.

TESS. Why would it?

EMMA. Remember my friend Aimes Lockhart from Weslyan?

TESS. No.

EMMA. He's like gay royalty in the publishing world and I met a friend of a friend of his, named Parker, at this event/fund raiser/save the gays thing who thought I rocked. And Parker is Lydia Freemantle's right hand man.

TESS. THE Lydia Freemantle? Fuck.

EMMA. Fucking fuck.

*(Lights up on **LYDIA FREEMANTLE** at a desk. She stares at **EMMA** for a long moment.)*

LYDIA. Fascinating.

EMMA. Oh?

LYDIA. Parker said you were fascinating. I said to Parker, have her write a little something up. But Parker said, "This is one you have to meet, to understand the full force of WHO SHE IS."

EMMA. Is that a compliment?

LYDIA. Ha.

EMMA. That's very kind of Parker, since I've only met him once.

LYDIA. First impressions are the only thing that matter.

(**LYDIA** *stands.*)

Sherry? Brandy? Or I have a lovely white from Cassis. It's impossible to get it in New York and I pay triple what it would cost in France but it reminds me of reckless teenage summers carrying on with silly Italian boys in their motor boats. Vroom. Vroom.

EMMA. Yes.

LYDIA. To what?

EMMA. The Italian wine...I mean French wine with Italian boys.

LYDIA. Ha.

(**LYDIA** *opens the bottle of wine as quickly as if she were a waiter.*)

EMMA. Actually...

(**LYDIA** *whips around.*)

LYDIA. Oh God! You're not in recovery? I haven't done something despicable – wouldn't be the first time. Do you need to call...your sponsor?

EMMA. No, God, no. I am not in recovery. Not. Yet. I've just been feeling off. So maybe no wine. Today.

(**LYDIA** *pours herself a glass. She sniffs the wine and sighs.*)

LYDIA. August. Bain du Soleil. Tiny Bikinis, I couldn't get away with anymore. *(She takes a sip.)* Fizzy water?

EMMA. Yes. Please.

(**LYDIA** *pours some fizzy water in to a glass. She takes a long sip of wine.*)

(**LYDIA** *looks at her watch.*)

EMMA. I really appreciate you listening to my ramblings, Lydia.

LYDIA. As they say, thank you for sharing.

EMMA. I wanted to write something up for you but I've been wanting to write something for so long.

LYDIA. For how long?

EMMA. I can't say for certain it's ever gone well. I mean. I've had some things. Short stories? Published.

LYDIA. Where?

EMMA. On line mostly. Small Magazines. Minute, really. I forget their names...

LYDIA. Bloody awful, writing.

EMMA. But I was riffing the night I met Parker at Aimes' event and he said I seemed to have something a story, a thing, a something that he thought you would get... respond to but...but...sitting here I feel...foolish.

LYDIA. Parker has an eye. He has his finger on things, that frankly, I am too old to keep my finger on. And Parker is almost without opinion.

EMMA. Umm...is that possible?

LYDIA. Parker brought me the mother daughter meth addiction memoirs. I said, lets just publish one book. The diary of a meth mom and in the same book, part deux, the daughter who had to cope with the meth mom. And Parker said. It's two books, Lydia. And BAM, we have TWO best sellers on our hands.

EMMA. So, Parker did have an opinion about the meth mom and daughter.

LYDIA. He had a sense of the market, different from the discernment of an opinion. He was spot on. And he senses you would sell well. I think he's right. And

THAT'S what it is all about, Emma. Supply and demand. I can make people demand what you supply. And thank god I am in America and I can say that sort of thing out loud.

(**EMMA** *raises her glass of water.*)

EMMA. To mass market marketing! Of books and people!

(**EMMA** *sits.*)

LYDIA. The book is the person, the person is the book. This is you: attractive, straight-forward and intelligently self deprecating. Chock 'o block full of style.

EMMA. Sometimes, I think that's all I have.

LYDIA. Ha. BUT…

EMMA. You don't like my shoes?

LYDIA. Ha. I am interested in YOU, not your novel. I want to know YOUR story. YOUR dreams. YOUR inner demons. I want to know the gory details of your crack up…

EMMA. Ups. That would be plural. But hasn't the educated, crazy girl been done to death? I mean, I feel like the Bell Jar was a genre definer…

LYDIA. YOU are Bell Jar in the city.

EMMA. Nuts in Jimmy Choos?

LYDIA. Ha. Exactly.

EMMA. But the novel, or rather the idea for the novel was about race, race in New York in the 21st century. And an unlikely romance, not a romance really but a moment of collision, of confusion and connection, a moment of connection and consequence. And I was wearing, I mean my character, my protagonist would wear Payless shoes…

LYDIA. But they would look like Jimmy Choos.

EMMA. My idea is fiction.

LYDIA. Emma darling, fiction is for writers.

EMMA. Believe it or not, I'm aware of what fiction means.

LYDIA. I publish some literary giants, Pulitzer Prize winners, literary war horses, and a marvelous aboriginal writer who is a shoo in for the Nobel this year. And do you know what they all have in common? They write. All the time. They have been writing since they could hold a pen. They live and breathe to construct a perfect sentence and they know how to use the semi colon correctly. Words are their life. Are words your life?

EMMA. I mean…yeah…sure. Yes. Stuff has happened and I have not written as much as I had hoped. I do write. Most days.

LYDIA. Good. If you want to be a novelist then keep doing that and come back to me in two years, five years, ten years…when you have cobbled together a book and I can take a look at it and maybe buy it for fifty grand. Write your Proustian moment about race and identity in New York that all comes together in an East Harlem Starbucks. Write your ode to James Joyce, a modern day Ulysses set amidst the racial divide that is contemporary Manhattan. Take a stab at a post millenial version of *Bonfire of the Vanities*. Please by all means do it, someone has to. I love a good literary read as much as the next head of a publishing house. At the weekend, I read a book all bout Guernesy, told in the first person by a cranky cow farmer. Not light fare but I felt sated after. I had been somewhere. Now, I don't ever need to go to Guernsey because I already know it inside out. That's what a good novel does. And I long to go on those imaginary journeys but I'm afraid I'm a minority.

EMMA. Really?

LYDIA. 185 novels were published by the major houses last year versus 250 memoirs. Do the maths.

EMMA. That's a lot of memory.

LYDIA. People feel the need to know that what they are reading is linked to some kind of absolute truth, whatever that might be.

EMMA. Since when did truth become so important?

LYDIA. Since the American imagination failed. The average reader can envision something if they believe it really happened. Make believe – too challenging.

EMMA. That's so sad.

LYDIA. A tragedy, really. Bottom lining it: I can sell you. Not your novel. Write a memoir. You'll make more money. I'll make more money. Get me a five page outline by Monday and I can have a mid six figure check in your bank account by Friday at the latest. Parker said money was of some concern to you.

EMMA. Yes. I mean, I am running out. I need, will need more money. At some point. Soon. I'm in a period of umm…transition. Big life change.

LYDIA. Exciting.

EMMA. And scary.

LYDIA. Five pages. Brief. Funny. You. Throw a little racial consciousness in there for good measure. Sure why not, it's your heart, I want to know your heart too, Emma.

EMMA. And what shoes I wear?

LYDIA. Tell me that and I'll cut the check myself.

(Lights come back up on **TESS***.* **EMMA** *gets up from the desk. Lights fade on* **LYDIA***.)*

TESS. Lydia Freemantle did not say that about your shoes!

EMMA. She said a lot more than that about my shoes. It's all we talked about, really.

TESS. She has this…this ravenous ambition that she somehow gets away with.

EMMA. Maybe because she's British. She's supposed to be polite but she isn't – but sort of sounds like she is.

TESS. Plastic surgery?

EMMA. Skillful Botox. Maybe a pinch of Restylane on her lips.

TESS. Couture?

EMMA. Vintage Chanel.

TESS. Fuck her.

*(**TESS**' phone rings. She looks at the number. She picks up. Monotone.)*

What? Then what happened? Then what? Then what? *(a long pause)* Where are they now? Yeah. Sounds right. I'm still with her. I'll come and get them all in the morning. I don't know. I don't know. I really have no idea. You run a multi-billion dollar company, figure it out.

*(**TESS** hangs up. A long pause.)*

Marie Antoinette is dead.

*(**TESS** begins to cry, softly.)*

*(**EMMA** looks confused. She wants to comfort **TESS**; she makes a move but doesn't know what to do.)*

She was supposed to be hopeful. Bring hope back. Marie Antoinette was supposed to bring hope back in to our miserable, dumb lives.

EMMA. I know I am out of touch and bad me for that, but who is Marie Antoinette? I mean, I know who she is.

TESS. *(weeping)* The fucking puggle.

EMMA. I thought she was called Maddie?

TESS. Nick name. My twins killed their dog.

EMMA. They thought it was a game, for sure, kids don't get death.

*(**TESS** gets up and gets vodka out of the fridge. There isn't much left.)*

TESS. I can't catch a break.

*(**EMMA** stands up and looks around nervously)*

EMMA. I'm sorry, Tess. Really sorry.

*(**EMMA** looks through the cabinets. She pulls down a bottle of Maker's Mark. She hold it up to **TESS**. **TESS** shrugs her shoulders. **EMMA** makes a bourbon on the rocks for **TESS**. She hands it to her. **TESS** sips it and stares into the distance. **EMMA** sits down. An awkward pause.)*

EMMA. Did you love Marie Antoinette?

TESS. She was a nightmare.

EMMA. Lived up to her name.

TESS. She shit everywhere, all over my antique Persian rugs and Fortuny upholstery – like messy, loose shits, the kind that you have to scrub and scrub but still leave flaming yellow rings. I got a dog whisperer in. He said I was too indulgent with her. Me? She slept in my bed. I mean, in it, under the covers with her head on a pillow. Harry and Charlotte could never get over it.

EMMA. Wow. I think I'm going to become an animal person.

TESS. Like the way people go to a spa for a weekend and come back Buddhist?

EMMA. People with animals have such moving stories. Maybe I should get a dog?

TESS. I'm worried about my kids.

EMMA. It couldn't have been intentional.

TESS. They did it once before. Marie Antionette had to take medicine to make her throw up.

EMMA. Maybe they missed you and they thought it was a good way to get you to come and whisk them to the vet and back to the safety of Westchester County.

TESS. I don't think they ever miss me.

EMMA. Stop.

TESS. I never give them the opportunity to wonder what it would be like without me. I call them even when they're with Steve. I text them. I call the nannies. At home when they're sleeping, I check on them, three times a night.

(**TESS**' blackberry rings. She looks at the number.)

It's Charlotte, the little Lizzie Borden of Duane Street.

(**EMMA** picks up the phone, turns it off and throws it in a drawer.)

EMMA. You've gone AWOL on Mulberry Street. You are mourning Marie Antoinette with your fucked up little sister.

(It is desperately quiet.)

TESS. My turn.

EMMA. Your turn to what?

TESS. To tell your story.

EMMA. How does that work?

TESS. My way.

EMMA. Which part of the story?

TESS. Getting ready for your date with Alejandro.

EMMA. Why that part?

TESS. Because I know that part.

EMMA. Have you suddenly become psychic now that your Puggle died?

TESS. I shared a bath room with you growing up.

EMMA. So?

TESS. I know how you prepare to conquer.

EMMA. The word conquer sounds way too Jackie Collins.

TESS. I thought this was a story about Incas. And if you talk about Incas the word conquest is on the table.

(Lights come up on **ALEJANDRO**. *He looks out, as if her were looking into a mirror.)*

He stared in the mirror in his apartment, while you debated in yours.

(Lights up on **EMMA** *holding up dress after dress in front of her. She drops one after another on to the floor.)*

You went home. You had to go home to debate, the kind of dress you would wear to dance with a guy waaay too young for you. While you wondered whether to be demure or hot, to wear black lace panties, or plain white cotton, he touched his face.

*(***ALEJANDRO** *touches his face.)*

He'd sprung for a razor that pivoted and gotten the closest shave of his life. He pondered whether to douse or not to douse with the Versace cologne his ex-girlfriend gave him for Christmas. Normally, he doused but he'd never been out with someone with a trust fund before and didn't know how they felt about cologne.

(**ALEJANDRO** *sniffs under his arms.*)

TESS. *(cont.)* He decided against cologne but applied an extra helping of Right Guard. He went for clean. You went for dirty.

(**EMMA** *slips on a tight, short clingy dress and puts on some light pink lipstick.*)

Dirty with clean makeup and a ponytail.

(**EMMA** *puts her hair back in a messy ponytail.*)

And both of you did what you have to do when you are about to venture out with someone completely wrong for you.

(**EMMA** *picks up a Gibson and drinks.* **ALEJANDRO** *gulps a beer.* **EMMA** *swigs the rest of her Gibson.* **ALEJANDRO** *finishes the last of his beer. They inhale deeply at the same moment. As they exhale, loud music plays, lights flash.* **EMMA** *waits.* **ALEJANDRO** *holds a beer and a bright green martini.*)

ALEJANDRO. I lost you.

EMMA. Not like I blend in, no I mean. I didn't mean that.

ALEJANDRO. I know you didn't. You don't. It's just.

EMMA. Just what?

ALEJANDRO. You look different.

EMMA. In a good way?

(**ALEJANDRO** *smiles. He hands* **EMMA** *the green martini. She looks at it but can't make herself sip it.*)

EMMA. I thought it would be different.

ALEJANDRO. The date?

EMMA. The club. Is this a date?

ALEJANDRO. I dressed like it was a date.

EMMA. You smell nice. Like laundry.

ALEJANDRO. Clean laundry, I hope?

(**EMMA** *smiles and looks at her drink again.*)

ALEJANDRO. So, this is different from other clubs you've been to?

EMMA. No. It's the same. I thought…

ALEJANDRO. What?

EMMA. That people would be salsa dancing, or something.

ALEJANDRO. I don't know how to do that kind of dancing but we can go to one of those clubs, if you want. I love the music.

EMMA. No…this is great.

(She toasts him with her drink.)

ALEJANDRO. The bartender didn't know what a Gielgud was.

EMMA. Gibson.

ALEJANDRO. What?

EMMA. Never mind this looks…divine.

*(**EMMA** finally takes a sip and forces a smile.)*

Mmmmm…sweet.

ALEJANDRO. It's an apple martini. I told them to put extra Midori in 'cause most girls like their drinks like cough medicine.

*(**EMMA** grabs **ALEJANDRO**'s beer and swigs it.)*

EMMA. Beer chaser. Woo-hoo!

ALEJANDRO. What's the antonym of Woo-hoo? Boo-hoo?

EMMA. Don't.

ALEJANDRO. Sorry.

*(**EMMA** finishes **ALEJANDRO**'s beer. She drops the beer and the martini glass and then pulls **ALEJANDRO** to her and kisses him. The music thumps as they kiss.)*

*(**TESS** watches them.)*

TESS. And you move into each other. And you move away, keeping the pulsing beat in your head, feeling fuzzy from the drinks but also achingly clear in your thoughts because what comes next is simple; it's the after that's the tricky part. It's the after, that'll kill you.

*(The music suddenly stops. Lights go down on **EMMA** and **ALEJANDRO**. **EMMA** gets up.)*

EMMA. Have you been watching a lot of Lifetime movies or something?

TESS. Good lay?

EMMA. Ew.

TESS. Was he a little Energizer bunny, or what?

EMMA. Stop it, Tess.

TESS. Did you do it here or at a hotel? He probably still lives at home. You didn't do it in his room with pictures of Lindsay Lohan everywhere?

EMMA. Lindsay Lohan is so a year and half ago, Tess.

(**EMMA** scours the cabinets for something.)

TESS. Are you looking for crack?

EMMA. Cookies. I have the cleaning lady hide them.

TESS. Of course.

EMMA. It's a strategy.

TESS. Do you always find them?

EMMA. Yes.

TESS. Then it's not an effective strategy. I mean what is the point…

EMMA. There is no point, Tess it is without a point at all, it is pointless like me, my life, my depraved sex life, my every thought and action. You win.

(**EMMA** finds a packet of chocolate digestive biscuits. She rips the packet open and devours a cookie.)

TESS. I seem to have struck a nerve.

(**EMMA** eats another cookie.)

You know what they say, you can't fill the void with food. The question you have to ask yourself is what is the emptiness about? (very calmly) I eat like you're eating when I think about the secret money Dad left you.

(**EMMA** eats another cookie. She coughs a little but keeps eating.)

He thought, he planned, he invested in that policy BEFORE I was even married to Steve.

EMMA. You were practically engaged.

TESS. 50% of marriages end in divorce.

EMMA. *(mouth full of cookie)* Maybe he just loved me more.

(**EMMA** *wipes the crumbs off of her dress. She dumps the remaining cookies in the trash. She ties up the trash and heads for the front door. The front door slams.*)

(**TESS** *looks at the drawer where* **EMMA** *put her phone. She walks toward the drawer and then walks away. She picks up one of the throw pillows from the couch and looks at the tag. She tosses the pillow down angrily. She marches toward the desk and takes her phone out and turns it on and makes a call.*)

TESS. *(monotone)* Hey. Right. Right. Right. Freezer seems like as good a place as any. Maybe you could put a pillow in there, a throw pillow under her head. *(a pause).* No. No. No. I do NOT think that is why this is happening. *(tone gets more animated)* Please! Please! Oh please You do that. You do that. Go right ahead.

(**EMMA** *enters.* **TESS** *does not see her.*)

Uh huh. Uh huh. Uh huh. Uh huh. WELL STEPHEN ABRAHAM STEIN… *(gets eerily calm)* Did you ever pause to think for a nanosecond that perhaps I slept with the goddamn au pair because ever since your fucking children were C-sectioned out of me, the sight of any part of my naked body made you cringe. Marie Antoinette is your fault. Harry and Charlotte are your fault. Everything that ever happens to me for the rest of fucking time is your fault you fucked up motherfucker.

(**TESS** *sees* **EMMA**.)

Gotta go.

(**TESS** *looks at* **EMMA**. *She doesn't know what to do with her phone.*)

I just. I just. I just. I just wanted to check in. Someone should just steal this from me, or cut my hands off, or fuse my fingers together.

(**EMMA** *takes the phone from* **TESS***. She puts the phone back in the drawer.*)

EMMA. Makes perfect sense.

TESS. What?

EMMA. That you're a lesbian. I remember the AU PAIR, she was Scandinavian, made great apple muffins. I mean, if I were a lesbian, I would want to be with a muffin maker too.

(**TESS** *laughs.*)

What?

TESS. Annika! Her. Me. I mean...she is SO not my type. She seems like she would spank you and then scrub you and then spank you some more.

EMMA. *(smiling)* Lesbian spanking isn't your thing? So, who is the non-spanker that exiled Steve from Westchester?

TESS. Jaap.

EMMA. Did you just bark?

TESS. The au pair's name is...was...is Jaap.

EMMA. Sorry, that just sounds wrong.

TESS. In the Netherlands it doesn't.

EMMA. Is it a girl's name?

TESS. Sorry to disappoint you. Jaap is a guy.

EMMA. You slept with a male Netherlandish au pair?

TESS. Dutch. Jaap was Dutch. He still is. If you're from the Netherlands you are Dutch.

EMMA. And where is Mr. Dutch Aupair now?

TESS. At the University of Groningen in Groningen. He's from Groningen.

EMMA. Is he getting his undergraduate degree at the university of Groan-again-and-again and again.

TESS. He wants to get his master's.

EMMA. But what degree is he CURRENTLY pursuing?

TESS. The Dutch prolong their educations forever.

EMMA. What about Jip.

TESS. Jaap. It's a long a.

EMMA. As I recall, you've had several au pairs since you had the twins and, if I remember correctly, all of them have been in the flush of youth. More often than not, they are recent high school grads, spending what I believe they call in Europe, a gap year, in the United States before they go to University, or in the case of Annika, cooking school.

TESS. Ingebord was 26.

EMMA. Is Jaap 26?

TESS. Well.

EMMA. It's a yes or no question.

TESS. No.

EMMA. Let me ask you this, is Jaap legal?

TESS. In the Netherlands.

EMMA. Here. Is Jaap legal here?

TESS. Legal?

EMMA. English is your first language. Yes or no.

TESS. Um…

EMMA. Wow. This changes everything.

TESS. Jaap…what happened between us…

EMMA. Unbelievable.

TESS. Don't.

EMMA. What?

TESS. Don't. Don't drag Jaap and me into your web of lies.

EMMA. My web of lies?

TESS. It's my life. I didn't write an autobiographical book claiming that I never fucked a nineteen year-old. *(beat)* He's twenty. Now.

(a pause)

EMMA. Would you have ever told me?

TESS. Probably not.

EMMA. Why not?

TESS. Because the whole thing made no sense.

EMMA. And I wouldn't be able to grasp the nonsensical?

TESS. I knew you would understand. I didn't want your empathy…I didn't want to be…

EMMA. You didn't want to be what?

TESS. Someone you could relate to.

EMMA. THAT is nonsensical.

TESS. I said that wrong.

EMMA. I get it Tess. I'm the crazy one, the sister who has to be put away every few years for months on end, in expensive clinics in inconvenient parts of the county. I'm the one who doesn't have a real job, or mate, or family. I am alone and weird and troublesome. And in every fiber of your being you want to be the opposite of me. I wonder if you would have any sort of a person- ality if it weren't for me? You expend so much energy being the "anti-me."

TESS. That is not true, Emma.

EMMA. For the first time in forever, you surprised me, you did something unexpected and out of character and DARING, yet you would go to any length to keep that from me, to omit that from the story. Isn't an omission really a lie, Tess?

TESS. It's not the same. I am NOT the same as…

EMMA. As me?

(a beat)

What was it like this morning when you opened up the paper and there I was. Your nutty little sis. Staring right back at you. Challenging you to DO something. Drastic. Dramatic. I knew you were coming over here before you even did. I planned what I would wear, down to my perfume and toe nail polish. I even put the Grey Goose in the fridge.

TESS. So this IS about hurting me?

EMMA. Don't flatter yourself, Tess. This is my story and you don't come into it until the end.

(Lights come up on **ALEJANDRO**. He holds out a paper bag to **EMMA**.)

ALEJANDRO. I bought ice cream. Vanilla. Chocolate. Strawberry. And then something with like nuts and cookie dough and peanut butter. I didn't know which way you swung...with ice cream. Like my mom'll only eat vanilla. Luis liked strawberry which I always thought was a little gay.

(**EMMA** *takes the bag and throws it in the freezer.*)

Not hungry. Makes sense. I'm not really hungry either. Maybe like you wanted something salty? I could get something. *(a pause)* Pretzels are good. *(longer pause)* I'm glad you called.

EMMA. I called you forty three times.

ALEJANDRO. My phone...

EMMA. What about your phone?

ALEJANDRO. *(looks around the apartment)* It looks nice here. You got some new furniture or something. It looks nicer. Different.

EMMA. It was a dump.

ALEJANDRO. No it wasn't. I mean, maybe for this neighborhood. Like what's the rent here? $1500?

EMMA. Why did you come?

ALEJANDRO. Uh...because you asked me to.

EMMA. I asked you before.

ALEJANDRO. I was crazy busy. Took the GED. It wasn't bad. Like you said, it wasn't bad.

EMMA. What made you come? This time.

(**ALEJANDRO** *looks really uncomfortable.*)

ALEJANDRO. Maybe I should come back. I can come back tomorrow. Bring pretzels. You can call me and tell me what you want.

EMMA. The cravings are over, Alejandro.

ALEJANDRO. I'm sorry.

EMMA. About what?

ALEJANDRO. You know...

EMMA. Say it.

ALEJANDRO. For not calling you back. You just sounded all weird and angry and I just got a lotta weird and angry in my life and...that's not even it.

EMMA. What is it, then?

ALEJANDRO. The last time...the last time, it was perfect and I wanted to remember it that way, not like everything always gets.

EMMA. Well, aren't you a romantic.

ALEJANDRO. I'm being real with you, Emma.

EMMA. Romance isn't real, Alejandro.

ALEJANDRO. That's just your mood talking.

EMMA. You make me feel old.

ALEJANDRO. You make me feel dumb.

EMMA. You're not dumb.

ALEJANDRO. Not that kinda dumb. I don't know what to do or say and I feel like I'm wrong for stuff I'm even thinking.

EMMA. Why did I think calling you would make me feel better?

ALEJANDRO. Because it was ours.

EMMA. It happens ALL the time. I'm not special or anything. This is not a unique experience. Just another dead thing, not even a person. Roadkill, really.

(beat)

ALEJANDRO. Maybe...maybe, it's for the best.

EMMA. History has proven again and again that no one can seem to save me from myself and my story does not have a fairy tale ending full of kids, cupcakes and childish hilarity. I don't get that story. All the cupcakes are for me and no one is laughing.

ALEJANDRO. Come on, Emma. This is one bad thing.

EMMA. You have no idea who I am!

ALEJANDRO. I know who you are.

EMMA. You don't know my story.

ALEJANDRO. I know you.

EMMA. You're just a…chapter, a not very interesting one at that.

ALEJANDRO. I feel fucking sad too. Shit like this doesn't happen to me every day.

EMMA. That's good to know.

ALEJANDRO. I'm not some asshole.

EMMA. Note taken.

ALEJANDRO. This means something to me too.

EMMA. Like you'll always wear a condom even if you're fucking a rich white girl?

ALEJANDRO. Jesus!

EMMA. Word to the wise: assume nothing about manic depressives, they can't be trusted.

ALEJANDRO. I can see how much you think of me.

EMMA. Mostly, I think about myself, Alejandro. It's part of my disease.

ALEJANDRO. You don't seem sick to me. Just pissed.

(**ALEJANDRO** *gets his jacket. As he leaves, he puts an envelope down on the kitchen counter. He exits.* **EMMA** *runs to the letter and rips it open.*)

ALEJANDRO. (*V.O.*) If it was a boy I would have named him Manco after the guy who was the king of the Incas and also god of the sun and fire because all those things together mean *poder* to me, which means power when you translate it.

(*Lights up on* **TESS** *listening to the letter as* **EMMA** *reads.*)

EMMA & ALEJANDRO. (*V.O.*) 'Cause his mother is full of strength and fire and all kinds of things that make me dizzy and also afraid. I would have told Manco to never be afraid of the things that make you dizzy but to hold on tight to them.

EMMA. If you don't, they slip away like a dream you forgot and then all you do is try to remember what you have lost.

(A moment. It feels long.)

TESS. That's very/ hard, I had a…

EMMA. /Don't. Pointed compassion, months too late, not so helpful.

TESS. I was just.

EMMA. People lose things, keys, ambitions, their minds.

TESS. Still.

EMMA. Loss is the same for everyone. It's what you do AFTER that's interesting and completely your own. I began to ask what if? What if my life actually meant something? Lydia convinced me I should write this idiotic book: "Bipolar with Style." But I just couldn't bear to write about my stupid real life. But then I began to think what if I had lead, said stupid life, but had overcome great odds to have it? What if I were me but better?

TESS. So, not really you.

EMMA. My struggles would make my excess and distress less…

TESS. Privileged.

EMMA. I was thinking more worthy of words.

TESS. More universal.

EMMA. Sure.

TESS. Maybe a best seller?

EMMA. Why not? And the more I wrote this other story, the more I believed it was the story that should have been who I was. It was an unconscious truth.

TESS. Ok. And let me guess, you write this quickly.

EMMA. Six weeks. More like five.

TESS. You were off your meds…You went off your meds when you found out you were pregnant. When was that?

EMMA. I can't recall.

TESS. You can't recall because you were in a manic haze. Was it before you met with Lydia?

EMMA. I am fully medicated at the present moment.

TESS. We are not talking about the present moment. We are talking about the crazy moments that make up the time you spent writing a totally fictional memoir.

EMMA. You haven't read it, you've just read ABOUT it.

TESS. Well, the blurb about being taken in by distant Incan East Harlem relatives after the untimely death of your vaguely Irish parents, gave me a taste of the imaginative quality of your work. Didn't you think you would be found out?

EMMA. If I am, I would argue: truth is a very relative concept these days. Reality television is scripted. Memoirs sell better than fiction but it is impossible to fact check memory. And Look at the evening news, its more entertainment than anything else. Truth and integrity don't matter in the world we live in.

TESS. Well, truth and integrity matter to me.

EMMA. You fucked your Dutch man au pair, ruined your marriage and irreparably damaged your kids. Were those the actions of a person of boundless integrity and honesty?

(**TESS** *is silent, perhaps for the first time ever. The buzzer rings.* **EMMA** *goes to answer it.*)

EMMA. Hello.

LYDIA. Lydia here. Can I come up?

(**TESS** *' jaw drops.*)

TESS. THE Lydia Freemantle. Why is she here? Oh shit.

EMMA. *(into the intercom)* Hey Lydia, come on up.

(*Both women freshen up in the mirror: they notice each other doing it and stop suddenly.*)

EMMA. She does that to people, makes you want to check your eye liner and reapply lipstick.

TESS. I didn't reapply.

EMMA. But you wanted to.

(The doorbell rings. **EMMA** *answers it. While,* **EMMA** *goes to the door,* **TESS** *looks closely at her lips in the mirror.* **LYDIA** *enters, dressed in a cocktail dress.)*

EMMA. Lydia…

LYDIA. Naughty. Naughty. Naughty.

EMMA. I've been meaning to call you back. I want to explain…

LYDIA. What's the Graham Greene quote…. "every writer has a splinter of ice in their heart." Yours is more of a glacier, darling. *(taking in* **TESS***)* Just tell me you are not a reporter.

*(***TESS** *is a little dumbstruck by* **LYDIA***.)*

TESS. Uh…

LYDIA. Was that a yes?

TESS. Uh…no. I'm…well I am a journalist.

EMMA. This is my sister, Tess.

LYDIA. Ah yes, I had a call from someone you work with at Good Housekeeping.

TESS. Luxurious Homes, actually. It's more of an Architectural Digest-type magazine.

LYDIA. This editor at not-quite-Architectural Digest was very upset about the Incas and your sister.

EMMA. Your editor called, Lydia?

TESS. I guess she was pissed. Because…she is Incan…I mean Quechuan or Quechua…I'm not sure what the adjectival form of the word is.

*(***LYDIA** *looks around the room.)*

LYDIA. I can see where your advance went. Nice coffee table.

EMMA.	**TESS.**
It's an Eva Zeisel.	Eva Zeisel makes such lovely and functional pieces.

TESS. Our mother worked for Zeisel. Assisted her, until she began designing her own work. I've been thinking about writing a book about her. Not Zeisel. Our mother.

LYDIA. That would probably be a different mother than the one who died of diabetes and smack in the "hood."

EMMA. In my book, we pick up with Paloma at the end of her story, the first half of her life is clouded in mystery. She is sort of a shadow figure. Tragic. Beautiful. Despairing. She could have, before her descent into heroin addiction, been a designer; I never say point blank, she DIDN'T design signature modernist furniture.

TESS. Our mother's name was Maureen. Maureen O'Donnell. Lydia, I just want you to know that I am as mortified as you are about this situation.

LYDIA. But I'm not mortified. *(beat)* Tess and Emma, how wonderfully 19th century of your parents. Seems to support the data that your father taught English literature at Sarah Lawrence and was not perhaps a part time bus driver/crack head.

EMMA. But, many of the characters in the book are based on people that I have encountered, who have no outlet to tell their stories. So, there IS a logic, a narrative of sorts.

LYDIA. I'm sure other writers have written packs of lies and masqueraded them as truth and not gotten caught. But you got caught.

EMMA. I didn't want to lie.

LYDIA. We are not *The New Yorker*, we can't fact check every last detail.

EMMA. I know.

LYDIA. And because you knew that you took advantage of the situation and violated the editor/author contract. I could have caused a stir when you delivered a completely different book than what we had agreed upon. But I didn't because you looked me in the eye and said your story was true. I had my doubts.

EMMA. Why didn't you voice them then?

LYDIA. It was a great read.

EMMA. It's a great read because the book is full of emotional truth.

LYDIA. As I am sure was James Frey's *A Million Little Lies.* Here is the thing: I love my job. And you seem to love spending the money my job gave you. So, if you want to hold on to your life and I want to hold on to my job, this is what we are going to do.

EMMA. There is more truth in this book than in most of the crap out there.

TESS. I think it's in your interest to listen to Lydia's plan.

EMMA. Since when have you become the mayor of my best interests?

TESS. I think if Lydia has an idea about how to solve this mess we should hear her out.

EMMA. There is no "we" in this situation.

LYDIA. Girls, girls, I have some ghastly thingy ma jiggy uptown, I haven't got all night.

TESS. Sorry, Lydia.

EMMA. You don't get to apologize to her.

LYDIA. So, we have documented proof that over the last fifteen years Emma has been institutionalized at least five times for bipolar disorder.

EMMA. I prefer "manic depressive."

LYDIA. So, we say this: the whole pitching, writing and publishing of your book was done while you were off your meds, which I want to assume is the truth.

TESS. It is the truth.

LYDIA. Basically your book is an ode to just how deluded someone who may suffer from delusions can get.

EMMA. I'm not delusional. That's not part of my illness.

LYDIA. The less you tell me the better.

TESS. That is brilliant.

LYDIA. I've got an expert reading the book right now; he has a Ph.D in everything and is willing to testify that you were not in your right mind when you wrote the book and that someone in your state could have indeed thought they grew up in the ghetto when in fact they grew up in an affluent Westchester suburb.

EMMA. But I was in my right mind.

LYDIA. I think that is a point for debate. Mind you, I don't want to be the one to debate it.

TESS.	EMMA.
I know what she gets like when she doesn't take her medicine.	Shut up, Tess. Stay out of this.

TESS. She doesn't sleep and so really the difference between being awake and dreaming is no different. I could testify, or rather support your expert's claims.

LYDIA. Perfect. The long suffering sister chimes in. Could be a book in that.

TESS. More like a trilogy.

EMMA. SHE is not a part of this story.

TESS. Once, one time, she ended up in jail in Tijuana with a gang of coke snorting Hell's Angels.

LYDIA. Too bad THAT didn't make it into THIS book.

TESS. I missed my graduation from Barnard because I had to go and bail her out.

EMMA. I will NOT write about TIJUANA!

(**EMMA** *sits down.*)

TESS. Come on, Emma. This is an out. It makes sense.

EMMA. I hate the crazy girl books. I would go so far as to say I disdain the Elisabeth Wurtzels and Susanna Kaysens of this world. "Girls interrupted on Prozac nation." Spare me the misery of that misery.

LYDIA. Fair enough. Let's just take a minute to go over the alternatives. Because you claimed to be telling me the truth and willfully lied to me and the publishing house; we'll stop printing on the book, fortunately it's not in stores yet, we'll pull the review copies, shame 'cause Michiko Kakutani ATE IT UP, and the house will ask for your advance back. And most probably, I will get fired for your lying. And because I am married to an extremely wealthy lawyer, I will sue you just for the fun of it and take every last farthing you have.

EMMA. Fine.

TESS. You don't mean that, Emma.

EMMA. I don't want to be the spokesperson for a disease, it's embarrassing.

LYDIA. More embarrassing than being plastered over Page Six and outed as an Inca poseur?

EMMA. Go ahead. Out me and take my coffee table while you're at it! Go on, please take my fucking coffee table!

LYDIA. Darling, if you don't do EXACTLY what I say, everything in this apartment will eventually be decorating my pool house in South Hampton.

EMMA. I'd be happier if I were homeless. Think of what a memoir that would make.

TESS. She's in a downward spiral. This is all a part of the disease.

EMMA. I've never felt so clear and sane in my entire life. Take the money. What's left of the advance and Dad's money too. (*to* **TESS**) Wouldn't you like me more if Dad's money just disappeared?

TESS. (*to* **LYDIA**) Excuse us Lydia, this is old family history and has nothing to do with you or this situation.

EMMA. History is something that's in the past. Dad's fucking money is in our face every minute.

(**EMMA** *gets up and searches in her handbag for a checkbook.* **EMMA** *writes a check.*)

(**EMMA** *hands* **LYDIA** *the check.* **LYDIA** *looks at the check and laughs.*)

LYDIA. Darling, this would barely cover my shoe habit for six months.

(**LYDIA** *rips up the check.*)

But I so appreciate the grand gesture. It would be so lovely if you could solve this problem with the scribble of a pen. But that sort of thing only happens in stories. I may have underestimated you, Emma. You might be a novelist yet.

EMMA. When I write my novel, you won't get to publish it.

TESS. Emma, Stop it.

EMMA. Shouldn't you get back to the twins before they poison the nanny or hang Steve in the playroom? (*to* **LYDIA**) Her twins murdered their dog earlier this evening.

TESS. That's unfair.

EMMA. And you trying to pawn me off to the public as a nut job is fair?

TESS. I am trying to save you from yourself.

EMMA. Not interested.

TESS. Fine.

(**TESS** *grabs her bag and walks toward the door. She turns around.*)

I quit.

(*She walks toward the door again and comes back.*)

And let me say, uttering those two words just lifted a weight off my shoulders, the unimaginable, impenetrable weight that is you, Emma. I never got to mourn, or lose my shit, or even be quiet after Mom and Dad. And really, that's all I want; a moment to think about the fucking tragedy that is my life. But no, there is always the crisis of you. The drama. The bad boyfriends. The blackouts. The schemes that reverberate with your fucked-up-ed-ness. I am bone tired of the ringing, clanging noise of you, Emma. I can't feel sorry for you anymore. Mostly, because all my caring and worrying and wondering has made you hate me. You did this, wrote these hurtful lies about our family to show me just how much you hate me, to show your disdain down my throat and make me choke on it. So. You win. I get it. I hate you back.

LYDIA. Right then.

TESS. I'm sorry you had to witness this, Lydia.

EMMA. Fucking make your exit, already.

(*TESS leaves. The door slams. A moment. LYDIA looks at her watch.*)

LYDIA. I've got a benefit. Breast cancer or Leukemia. Something everyone's dying of.

(*a pause*)

Tricky business – siblings. I haven't spoken to mine in ten years. I'm not a monster, you know.

EMMA. What are you then?

LYDIA. I've just learnt to market to people's inner monsters – to give the public as much "truth" as they can possibly bear. Don't know quite what you call someone who does that.

EMMA. Monster sounds right.

LYDIA. A reporter from Gawker will call you in the morning, tell them the story, whichever one it is. I'll see you in my office or some place where expensive lawyers congregate.

(*LYDIA leaves. EMMA is alone. She goes to her laptop and starts typing.*)

(*Lights shift. ALEJANDRO appears from the bathroom in a towel. He dries his hair.*)

EMMA. How was the shower?

ALEJANDRO. Almost bruised me it was so strong.

EMMA. I think it's environmentally incorrect.

ALEJANDRO. Wish you had been in there with me.

(*He kisses the back of her neck. EMMA smiles but keeps typing.*)

EMMA. I have a confession.

ALEJANDRO. You're not into Latino guys?

EMMA. I hate showering with someone else.

ALEJANDRO. Get out! But like last night in the shower... that didn't seem like hate. *(beat)* You weren't faking?

(**EMMA** *looks up from her computer.*)

EMMA. No! I mean, No. It's just...It would be just as good on the bed, or the sofa.

(**ALEJANDRO** *looks at the sofa.*)

ALEJANDRO. That sofa is too nice to get nasty on.

EMMA. I always feel like I might slip and fall in the shower. More household accidents happen in the bathroom than anywhere else.

ALEJANDRO. Is that what you were thinking about last night?

EMMA. No!

ALEJANDRO. Come on...Emma-Lemma ding dong, I want the truth, the whole truth and nothing but the truth.

EMMA. Ok. I thought about it for a second. *(beat)* Maybe two.

ALEJANDRO. And I thought all that moaning and groaning was about me. Turns out, you were re-enacting your head splitting open.

(**EMMA** *gets up from her computer.*)

EMMA. You hungry?

ALEJANDRO. I'm always hungry.

EMMA. I can make some pasta.

ALEJANDRO. Can you make anything else?

EMMA. Pasta or take out.

ALEJANDRO. Pasta. Just don't make me eat any of that raw fish again.

EMMA. You will acquire a taste for sushi, if it kills me.

ALEJANDRO. If you start digging it in the shower, I'll eat that maki/haki shit.

(EMMA gets up and starts getting things together for dinner in the kitchen.)

(ALEJANDRO leafs through some papers on EMMA's desk. He plops down at her computer and reads from the screen. EMMA holds up a jar of tomato sauce and a jar of pesto.)

EMMA. Pesto? Or Tomato sauce?

ALEJANDRO. *(reading)* Tomato.

EMMA. Farfalle or Buccatini?

ALEJANDRO. *(still reading)* Don't know what either is, so I guess it don't matter.

(EMMA thinks.)

EMMA. Buccatini it is. My mom made this incredible pasta with buccatini. It was a Carbonara but instead of using bacon, she used pancetta; it was salty and creamy and Tess and I loved it so much we would beg for thirds. I think once I ate so much, I threw up. You ever done that?

ALEJANDRO. *(still reading)* What?

EMMA. Been a complete pig?

ALEJANDRO. *(looks up)* With pretty much everything.

(He goes back to reading.)

EMMA. My mom could make the simplest thing tasty, like even her peanut butter and jelly was special. She did that in her work too. I should show you some of the pieces she designed…There's a book. Not a whole book. It's a book about modern women designers.

ALEJANDRO. *(reading)* Clothes?

EMMA. Furniture. People always describe her work as "harmonious," which truth be told is a kind of cheesy word but she was one of those people. Sorta the opposite of me. What's the antonym of harmonious? Discordant? That's an apt description of me AND Tess. We're like that modern classical music that gives you a headache. Mom was more of a Bach sonata.

(ALEJANDRO looks up.)

ALEJANDRO. What is this?

EMMA. What?

(ALEJANDRO points to the computer.)

EMMA. A story.

ALEJANDRO. About who?

EMMA. No one in particular.

ALEJANDRO. *(reading)* "Frederico had a certain power in the bedroom that he lacked in life. It's as if the Gods of Cusco and Machu Pichhu came to him when he fucked. His cock was the sun and I worshipped it and would have sacrificed my very soul for a taste of it. Out of the bedroom, he wasn't a God, not even God-like. This was a disappointment." What the fuck?

(EMMA holds up a bottle of red wine and a bottle of white wine.)

EMMA. Red or white?

ALEJANDRO. Is that what you think?

EMMA. Do you want a beer? Or can I make you a scotch?

(ALEJANDRO charges toward her knocks the wine glass out of her hands on to the floor.)

ALEJANDRO. Fucking look me in the eye and tell me that I am not a disappointment.

EMMA. It's a story.

(ALEJANDRO begins to pace around the apartment like a caged animal.)

ALEJANDRO. Nah uh. Nah uh. No way. Not after last night. You said that stuff. We did the whole God/fucking Inca thing, which I wasn't that into. Me? I like a straight simple fuck. But white girls need a lot of talking and game playing and as long as I get some, whatever. I've done dumber things for pussy.

EMMA. Stop, Alejandro.

ALEJANDRO. You wanna play it like that. Like I'm some boy fucking toy, some brown notch in your belt I can do it. But let's make it more interesting.

(**ALEJANDRO** *kicks the sofa. He pushes the coffee table with his foot, he knocks books off the bookshelf.*)

EMMA. No one will ever see it.

ALEJANDRO. Come here.

(**EMMA** *doesn't move.*)

EMMA. It's just thoughts, Alejandro. Thoughts are different from feelings.

ALEJANDRO. Fucking shut up and come over here. NOW.

(**EMMA** *walks toward* **ALEJANDRO.**)

ALEJANDRO. We're gonna do it MY way. My fucking disappointing way.

(**ALEJANDRO** *looks at the coffee table.*)

This coffee table expensive?

(**EMMA** *nods her head yes.*)

Cool. I am gonna fuck you on this expensive coffee table until it breaks in two. And you are gonna be quiet as a mouse. I'm not an Inca. I'm not a God. I'm just a boy from Uptown getting some.

(**ALEJANDRO** *shoves* **EMMA** *on the table. Lights shift.* **EMMA** *lies on the table.*)

(*Lights Fade.* **ALEJANDRO** *exits.*)

(*A door slams.* **EMMA** *sits upright.* **TESS** *enters.*)

TESS. You shouldn't lie on the Zeisel.

EMMA. I was trying to write a happy ending.

(**TESS** *goes to the desk and gets her phone.*)

TESS. Phone.

(**TESS** *heads for the door.*)

EMMA. I couldn't. Write a love story. Not even in my head. I made it ugly. It wasn't ugly.

TESS. I'm not really here.

EMMA. I can't even imagine a happy ending.

TESS. I am not really talking to you.

EMMA. Are you a delusion? Illusion? Contusion?

TESS. Don't start with the word games.

EMMA. You can't boss me around if you're not here. *(beat)* I thought I could rewrite myself. I wanted to believe that was possible.

TESS. It isn't.

EMMA. If you can't change your story, what's the point?

TESS. No idea.

EMMA. But if circumstances obstinately refuse to let you be happy you have the moral obligation to imagine a Hollywood ending. Dorothy gets back to Kansas. Cary Grant gets the girl. The phoenix MUST rise from the ashes.

TESS. What can I say, life is shitty. People are shitty. I'm shitty. I did it.

EMMA. Did what?

TESS. I got my editor to call Lydia. She wasn't even that angry. Sometimes, she doesn't admit to being Peruvian. Says she's Italian. I think she's Italian/Peruvian. Confusing. She didn't really care.

EMMA. You outed me?

TESS. I just I just…wanted you to get caught, for there to be consequences for your crazy actions. Just once.

(EMMA begins to laugh.)

What? Stop. It's NOT funny. You have to see my point, one time, once I do something, one thing. I have an affair, which…is a pretty banal thing in the scheme of treacherous things that go on the world and my life is fucked. Done. Nothing but consequences. My kids hate me. They killed my dog. It wasn't a mistake. It was a punishment. So. Yeah. I wanted you to be as fucked as me.

(TESS begins to leave.)

EMMA. Look around, Tess. This room. The exposed brick. The tasteful coffee table and well appointed throw rug are all about consequences. I thought, I thought if I made this place just a little bit beautiful, a tad bit... harmonious then maybe, just maybe I wouldn't have to live alone in it. I could share it. With someone. That's all I wanted. A life with someone who wouldn't vanish. Silly Emma. She doesn't get that story. And it's all her fault.

TESS. It's not your fault

EMMA. I'm alone. And I don't see that changing. I mean, I don't even want to be with me.

(a moment)

TESS. I. I. I don't want to go home to Westchester.

*(***TESS*** *and* ***EMMA*** *look at each other for a long moment.)*

*(***EMMA*** *goes to the freezer and pulls out a carton of sorbet. She gets two spoons and sits on the sofa.)*

(She offers a spoon to ***TESS.*** ***TESS*** *sits beside* ***EMMA*** *on the sofa. It's uncomfortable but familiar at once. The sisters eat sorbet.)*

"They fuck you up, your mum and dad. They may not mean to, but they do. They fill you with the faults they had And add some extra, just for you."

EMMA. "Man hands on misery to man. It deepens like a coastal shelf. Get out as early as you can, And don't have any kids yourself."

TESS. Philip Larkin got it.

EMMA. You ever think it was weird that was Dad's favorite poem?

TESS. It's a great poem. It was weird he made us memorize it.

EMMA. Is it true?

TESS. Kinda.

EMMA. Didn't seem true when I was pregnant.

TESS. The hormones con you.

EMMA. But Harry and Charlotte, they changed you?

TESS. Do I look like a phoenix in ruby slippers to you? I wish it wasn't sorbet.

EMMA. In the novel version, it'll be hazelnut gelato.

TESS. And we'll be pear shaped and despairing.

(beat)

I've been thinking.

EMMA. Uh-oh.

TESS. I think about other people besides you. I wonder if Steve and I should share custody of the twins.

EMMA. Wow.

TESS. I'm not sure I know how to make them happy, Em. Maybe he does. Is that selfish?

EMMA. I think it's...noble.

TESS. Really?

EMMA. Maybe noble and selfish aren't so far apart.

TESS. Maybe we could try... never mind.

EMMA. What?

TESS. To be selfish in the right way. Together.

EMMA. But we've never done anything together.

TESS. We've endured, Emma.

EMMA. Tess, I don't want to publish any memoir, ever.

TESS. Ok.

EMMA. That's it?

TESS. That's it. I get it. You. This not-memoir-that-will-never-be. I wanna new, fake, true story too. If I could think of one, I would.

EMMA. It all starts with two little words. What if?

TESS. What if?

EMMA. What if we had been born to parents who were not extraordinary in any way –

TESS. And they weren't smart or charming and they loved US more than each other.

EMMA. What if our wildly normal parents loved us rightly.

TESS. Equally.

EMMA. What if we grew up knowing that whatever happened we could lean on the other.

TESS. Even if our loving parents were suddenly killed or taken ill. The good love would live on between us and grow and turn into the kind of love you pass on.

EMMA. The kind of love that doesn't die, even though people do.

(beat)

TESS. So, love doesn't die?

EMMA. I want to believe it lasts and lasts.

TESS. Me too.

EMMA. Is this our happy ending?

TESS. You're the writer.

EMMA. I write, I'm not a writer.

TESS. You are a writer. Write. Fiction.

(The sisters glance at one another. They look out. A long, almost calm moment. They sigh at the same moment.)

EMMA. Yeah.

TESS. Yeah.

(Lights slowly fade as the sisters take in this new world order.)

End of Play

Also by
Cusi Cram...

Dusty and the Big Bad World

Fuente

Lucy and the Conquest

OTHER TITLES AVAILABLE FROM SAMUEL FRENCH

DUSTY AND THE BIG BAD WORLD

Cusi Cram

Comedy / 1m, 3f, 1 girl

Dusty and his animated friends hold a competition to find a model family based on letters written by children. The winning family will receive a visit from Dusty and will be filmed for an upcoming episode. Out of the 15,000 letters received, the producers pick Lizzie Goldberg-Jones and her family to be featured on the most popular animated PBS show in America. Her parents are exemplary role models – and they are two men. When word of that selection and the resulting episode reaches Marianne, Secretary of Education, she exercises her authority, deciding that the program should not be aired on public television because of its possible influence on children. Her decision, calling the episode "special interest TV", is a blow to Jessica and Nathan, the producers/writers of the show and to Karen, Marianne's secretary. Karen admires her boss' tenacity in overcoming a self-destructive past, but feels her decision to cancel the episode is definitely wrong. She secretly reveals that self-destructive past to Nathan and almost brings Marianne down, but not quite. Based on an actual incident that happened in 2005, *Dusty and the Big Bad World* is a very funny, no-holds-barred yet even-handed look at PBS, government bias, gay marriage, the right to privacy, children's allergies and the ability to survive in a small-minded world.

OTHER TITLES AVAILABLE FROM SAMUEL FRENCH

FUENTE

Cusi Cram

Dramatic Comedy / 4m, 2f

Something is not right. There is a secret humidity in the air in a town where the breezes have been on strike for two hundred years. Soledad thinks she is Alexis Carrington from Dynasty and feels itchy. Chaparro can't seem to scratch her itch anymore. Esteban might just be the man for the job. And Adela watches it all unfold as if it were a soap opera on TV. Maybe it is? Anything is possible in Fuente, an almost-real town, somewhere between where North America ends and South America begins.

Fuente is a magically-real comedy set in a remote desert town about love, revenge, escape, and the perilous powers of Aquanet hairspray.

"The play, *Fuente*, is powerful, moving and original, which after a three-year development process and a Herrick Theatre Foundation Prize for New Play, is being given a smartly staged, well acted world premiere at Boyd's smaller venue in Sheffield. Cram has written a small-scale at once real and mythical epic about love, vengeance and one's sense of place. The language is earthy (this is NOT a family show!) and poetic. The characters and their stories are sad but also funny enough to have the audience burst out laughing. The Garcia Marquez-like magic is amusingly propelled by a bottle of Aqua Net hair spray."
– *CurtainUp.com*

SAMUEL FRENCH STAFF

Nate Collins
President

Ken Dingledine
Director of Operations,
Vice President

Bruce Lazarus
Executive Director,
General Counsel

Rita Maté
Director of Finance

ACCOUNTING

Lori Thimsen | Director of Licensing Compliance
Nehal Kumar | Senior Accounting Associate
Charles Graytok | Accounting and Finance Manager
Glenn Halcomb | Royalty Administration
Jessica Zheng | Accounts Receivable
Andy Lian | Accounts Payable
Charlie Sou | Accounting Associate
Joann Mannello | Orders Administrator

BUSINESS AFFAIRS

Caitlin Bartow | Assistant to the Executive Director

CORPORATE COMMUNICATIONS

Abbie Van Nostrand | Director of Corporate
Communications

CUSTOMER SERVICE AND LICENSING

Brad Lohrenz | Director of Licensing Development
Laura Lindson | Licensing Services Manager
Kim Rogers | Theatrical Specialist
Matthew Akers | Theatrical Specialist
Ashley Byrne | Theatrical Specialist
Jennifer Carter | Theatrical Specialist
Annette Storckman | Theatrical Specialist
Julia Izumi | Theatrical Specialist
Sarah Weber | Theatrical Specialist
Nicholas Dawson | Theatrical Specialist
David Kimple | Theatrical Specialist
Ryan McLeod | Theatrical Specialist

EDITORIAL

Amy Rose Marsh | Literary Manager
Ben Coleman | Literary Associate

MARKETING

Ryan Pointer | Marketing Manager
Courtney Kochuba | Marketing Associate
Chris Kam | Marketing Associate

PUBLICATIONS AND PRODUCT DEVELOPMENT

Joe Ferreira | Product Development Manager
David Geer | Publications Manager
Charlyn Brea | Publications Associate
Tyler Mullen | Publications Associate
Derek P. Hassler | Musical Products Coordinator
Zachary Orts | Musical Materials Coordinator

OPERATIONS

Casey McLain | Operations Supervisor
Elizabeth Minski | Office Coordinator, Reception
Coryn Carson | Office Coordinator, Reception

SAMUEL FRENCH BOOKSHOP (LOS ANGELES)

Joyce Mehess | Bookstore Manager
Cory DeLair | Bookstore Buyer
Kristen Springer | Customer Service Manager
Tim Coultas | Bookstore Associate
Bryan Jansyn | Bookstore Associate
Alfred Contreras | Shipping & Receiving

LONDON OFFICE

Anne-Marie Ashman | Accounts Assistant
Felicity Barks | Rights & Contracts Associate
Steve Blacker | Bookshop Associate
David Bray | Customer Services Associate
Robert Cooke | Assistant Buyer
Stephanie Dawson | Amateur Licensing Associate
Simon Ellison | Retail Sales Manager
Robert Hamilton | Amateur Licensing Associate
Peter Langdon | Marketing Manager
Louise Mappley | Amateur Licensing Associate
James Nicolau | Despatch Associate
Emma Anacootee-Parmar | Production/Editorial
Controller
Martin Phillips | Librarian
Panos Panayi | Company Accountant
Zubayed Rahman | Despatch Associate
Steve Sanderson | Royalty Administration Supervisor
Douglas Schatz | Acting Executive Director
Roger Sheppard | I.T. Manager
Debbie Simmons | Licensing Sales Team Leader
Peter Smith | Amateur Licensing Associate
Garry Spratley | Customer Service Manager
David Webster | UK Operations Director
Sarah Wolf | Rights Director

SAMUELFRENCH.COM
SAMUELFRENCH-LONDON.CO.UK